There are many versions of this classic tale. In the tradition of the storyteller, each one is uniquely different.

Library of Congress Cataloging-in-Publication Data

José, Eduard.
  [Cabellos de oro.   English]
  Goldilocks and the 3 bears / illustration, José
M. Lavarello ; adaptation, Eduard José ; retold
by Janet McDonnell.
      p. cm. — (A Classic tale)
  Translation of: Cabellos de oro.
  Summary: Lost in the woods, a tired and
hungry girl finds the house of the three bears
where she helps herself to food and goes to sleep.
  ISBN 0-89565-465-2
  [1. Folklore.   2. Bears—Folklore.]
I. Lavarello, José M., ill.   II. McDonnell, Janet,
1962-   .   III. Three bears.   IV. Title.
V. Title: Goldilocks and the three bears. VI. Series.·
PZ8.1.J75Go   1988   398.2'1—dc19 [E]   88-36870
                                           CIP AC

© 1988 Parramón Ediciones, S. A.
Printed in Spain by Sirven Gràfic, S. A.
© Alexander Publishers' Marketing
and The Child's World, Inc.: English
edition, 1988.
L.D.: B-41.153-88

A CLASSIC TALE

Goldilocks
and the 3 Bears

Illustration: José M. Lavarello
Adaptation: Eduard José

Retold by Janet McDonnell

The Child's World, Inc.

Once upon a time, there lived a little girl whose hair was so fair, her mother called her Goldilocks. Goldilocks was beautiful, but more than that, she was kind and polite. She had such a good heart that everyone in the village loved her. When she walked down the street, people leaned out of their windows to greet her.

"Hello, Goldilocks," they would say.

And she would answer with a smile, her golden hair shining in the sun.

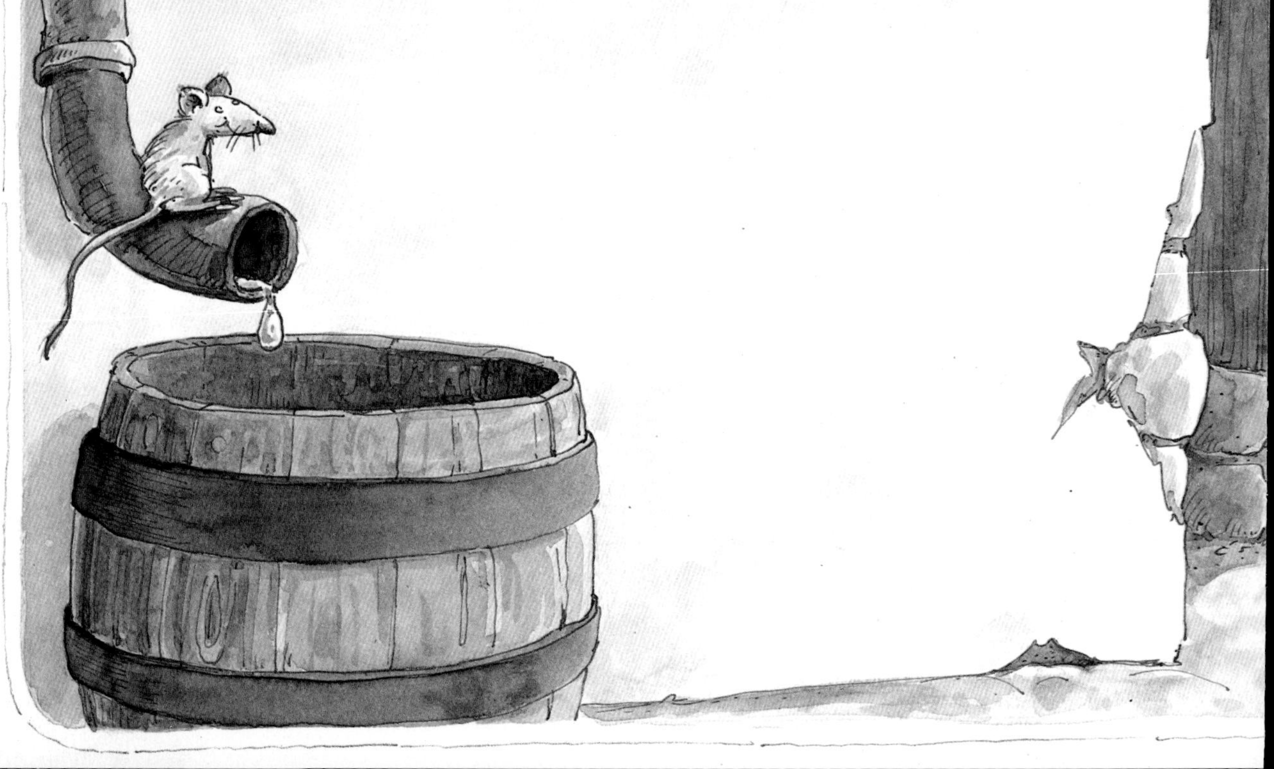

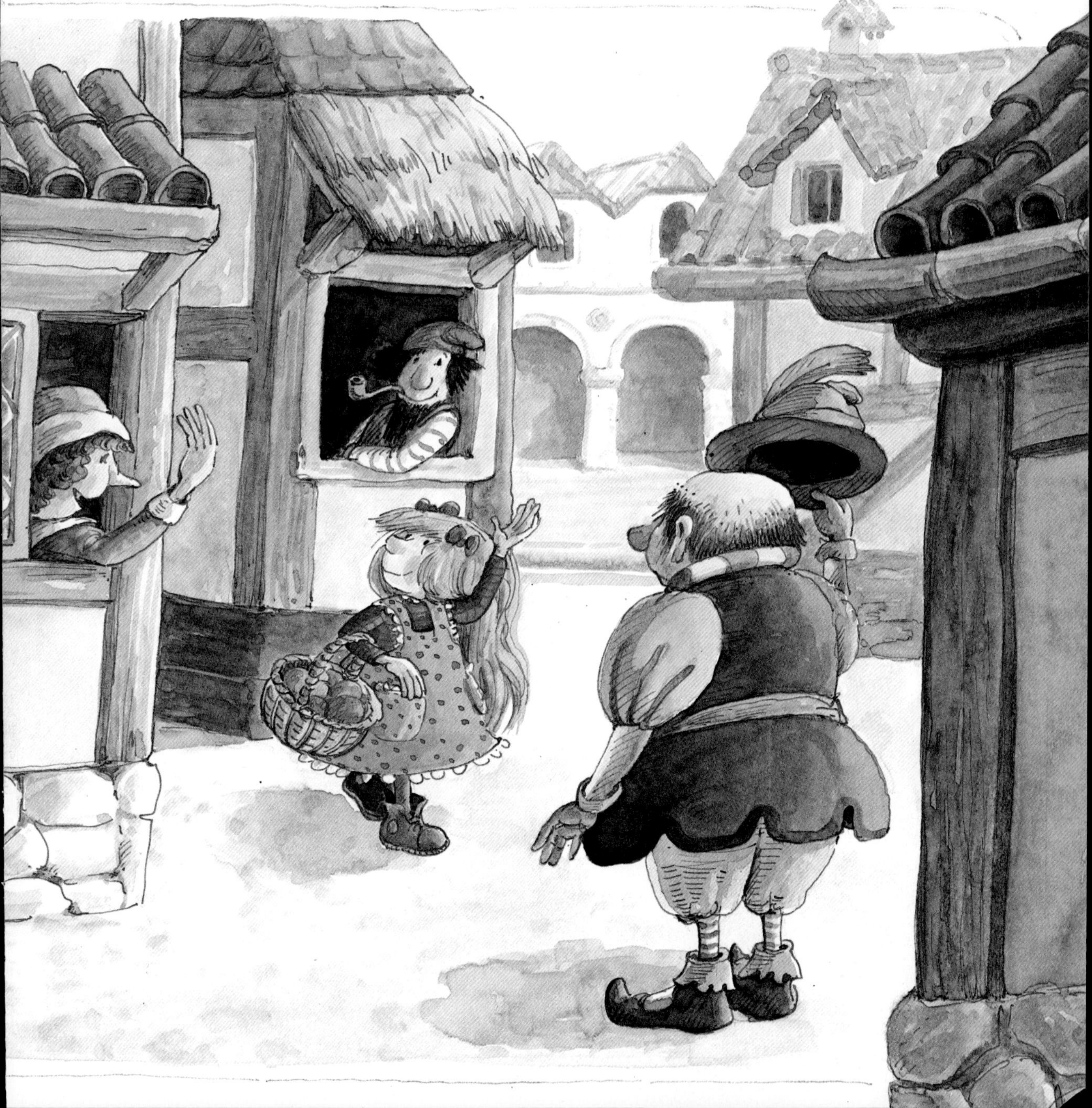

One evening Goldilocks was having supper with her mother when she remembered something.

"Mother, do you know why Paul's parents have forbidden him to go to the woods?"

"Because people say the woods are full of danger," answered her mother.

"What kind of danger?" asked Goldilocks.

"No one knows for sure," her mother said. "But everyone says it is a dangerous place. You must stay away from there."

Goldilocks said no more. But she was curious about the woods. What strange things were hidden there? For the rest of the day, she could think of nothing else.

"It can't be so bad to go walking there," she said to herself. "There is nothing but trees, plants, and animals in the woods. In the picture books the woods are always beautiful."

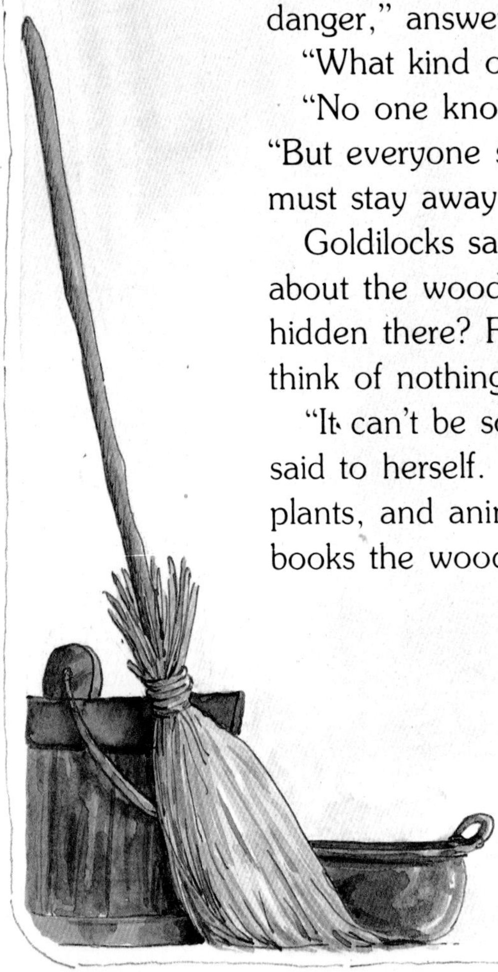

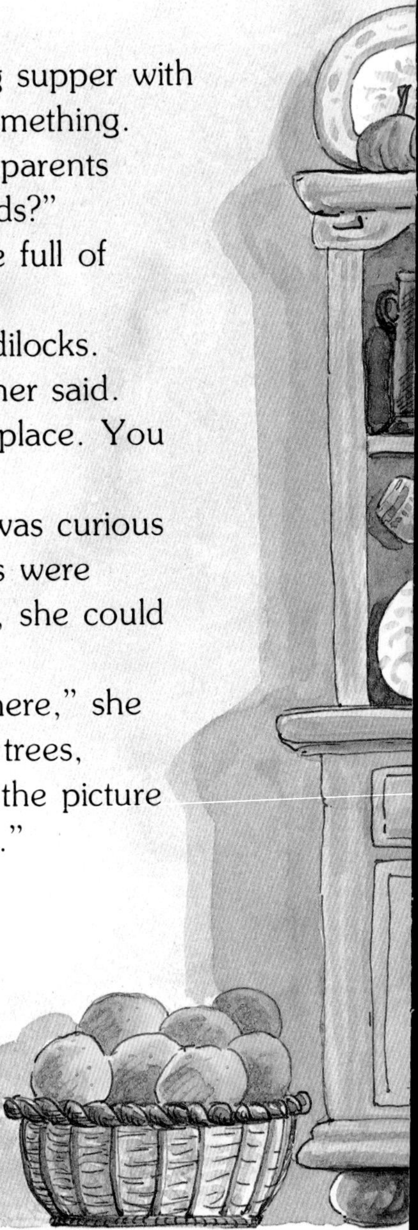

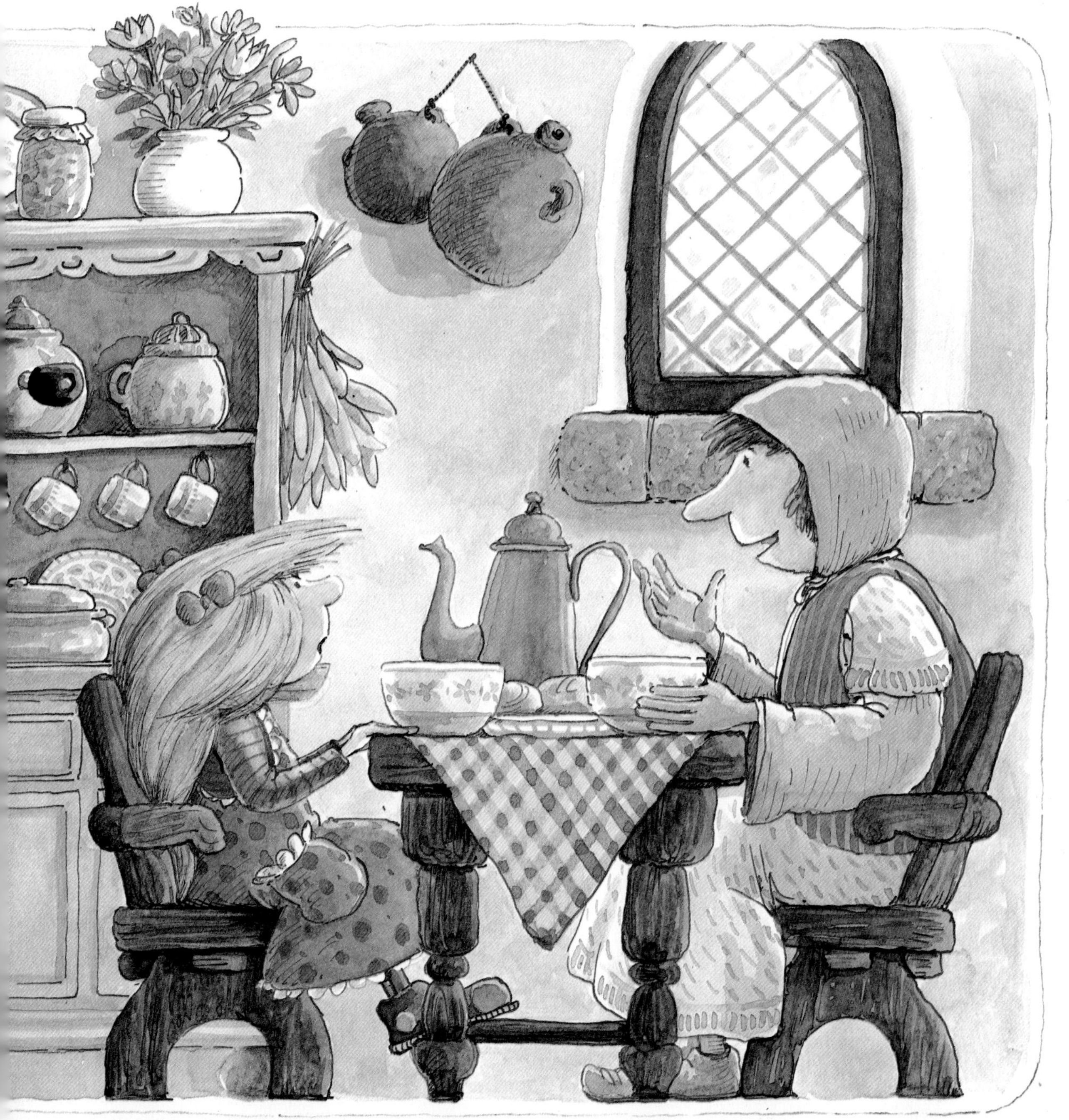

The next day, Goldilocks did something she had never done before. She disobeyed her mother.

"I'm going to play at Alice's," she said. But instead, she headed for the woods.

"I just want to take a little look," she thought. "I won't be gone long."

As she passed the blacksmith's house, he called out to her, "Good morning, Goldilocks. You're not thinking of going to the woods, are you?"

"Oh no," she answered.

"Good," he said. "It's dangerous there."

But his warning only made her more curious.

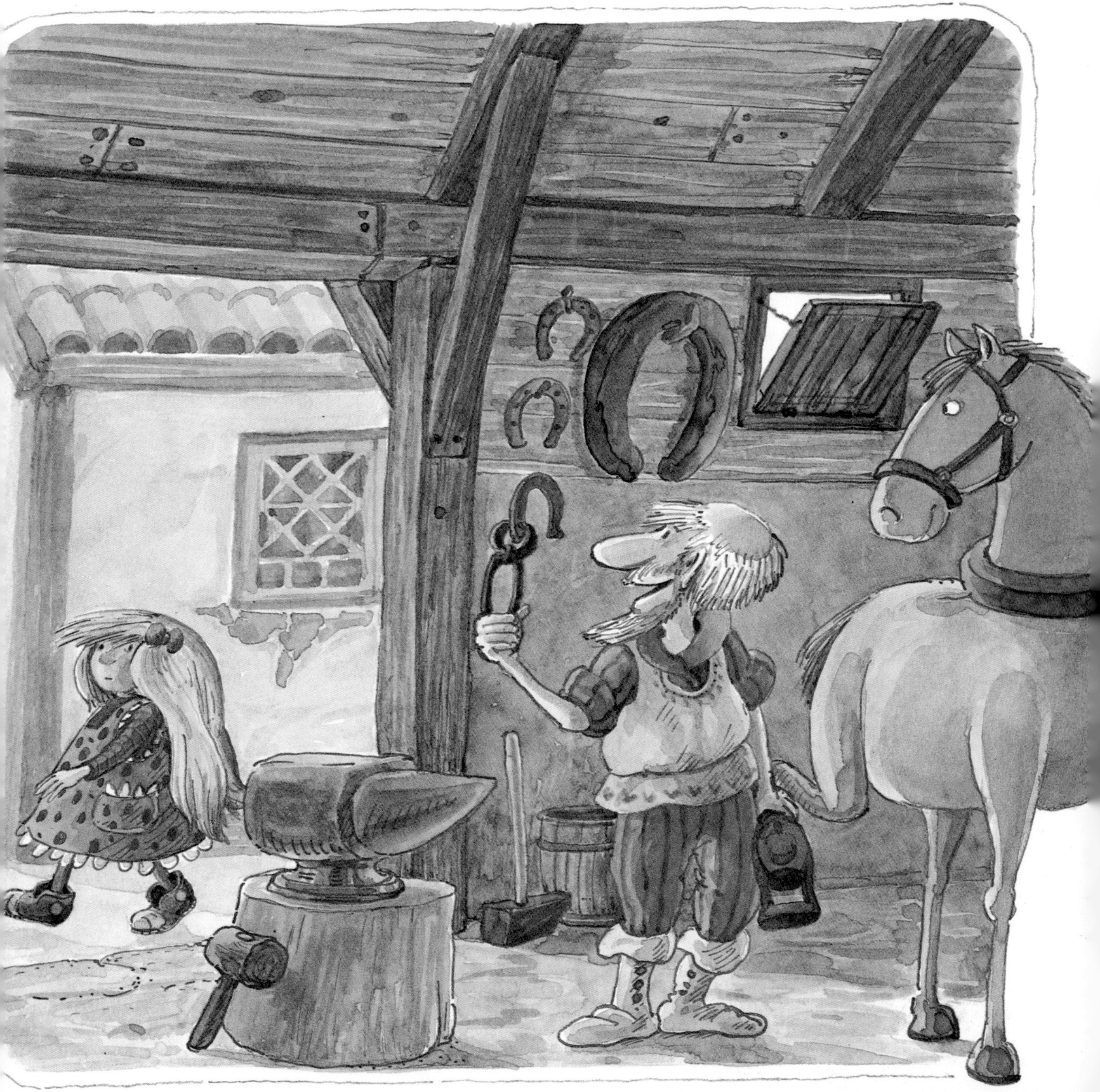

Soon she reached the edge of the woods. The trees were so tall and the birds sang so sweetly. Everything was cool and green.

"How pretty!" said Goldilocks.

The little girl skipped along, singing a song, and following a road deep into the woods. Little squirrels hid in the trees, flowers proudly showed their colors, and sunlight danced upon the leaves. There were so many things to see!

"My mother was wrong!" said Goldilocks. "This is a beautiful place!"

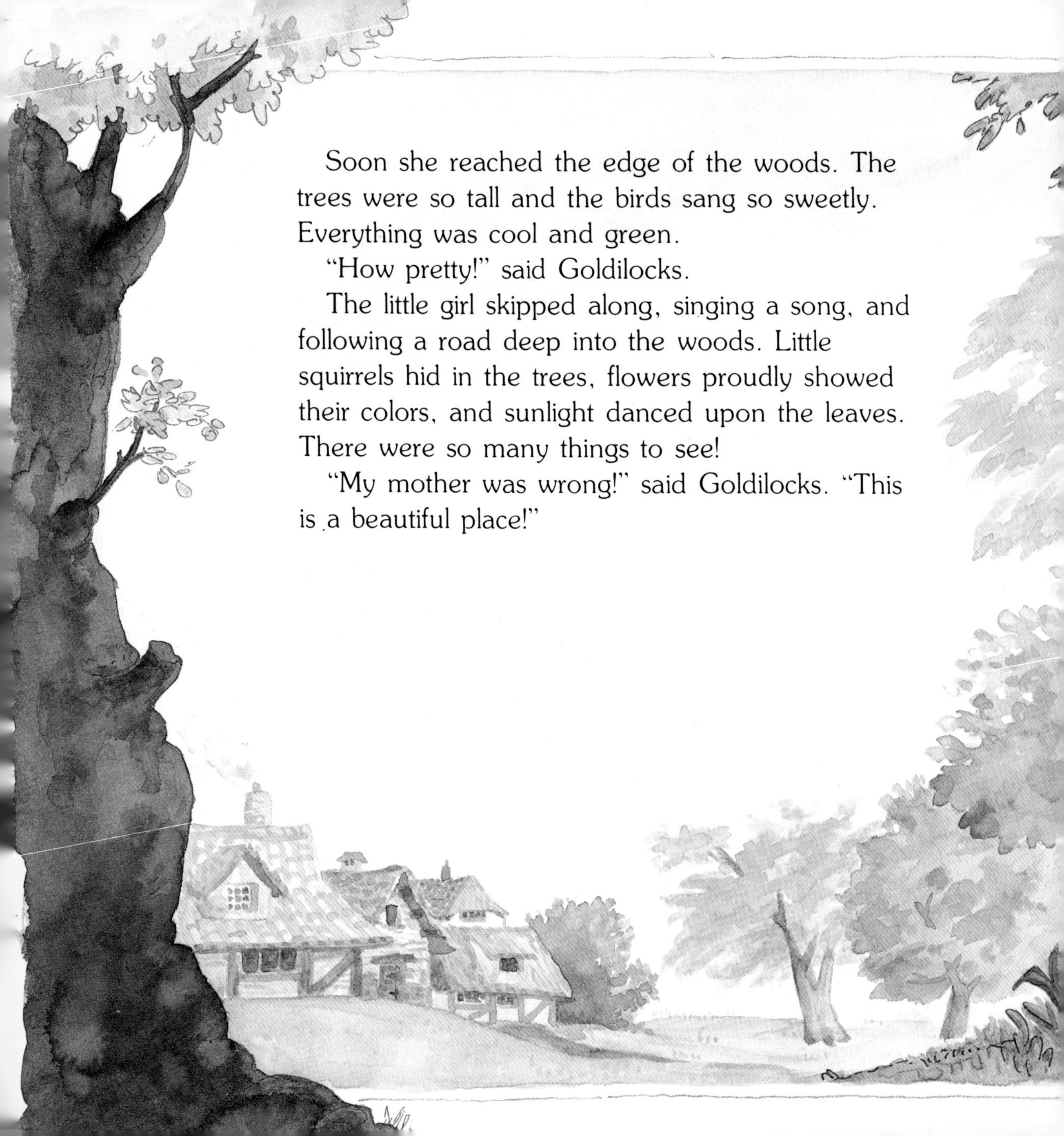

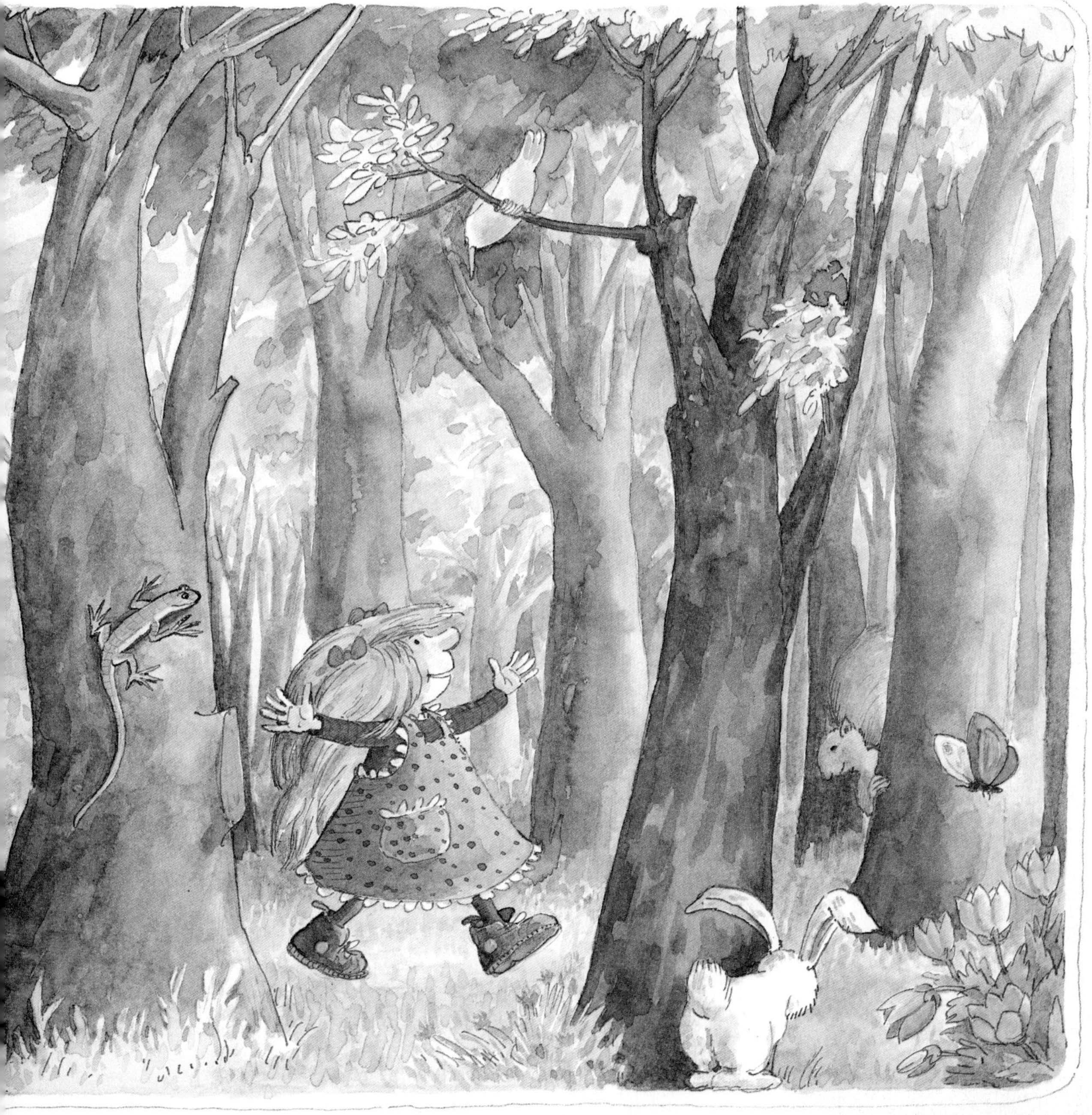

She was having such fun that she didn't think about how far she had come. But suddenly, she felt very hungry.

"Maybe I should go back," she said to herself. "The people in the village will wonder where I am."

But when she turned around, she saw the roof of a house behind a cluster of trees.

"The woods *must* be safe if people live here!" she said. She began walking toward the house. "I'll ask them for a drink of water. The sun has made me thirsty."

It was a friendly-looking house, not too big and not too small. Goldilocks walked up to the door and found that it was not locked.

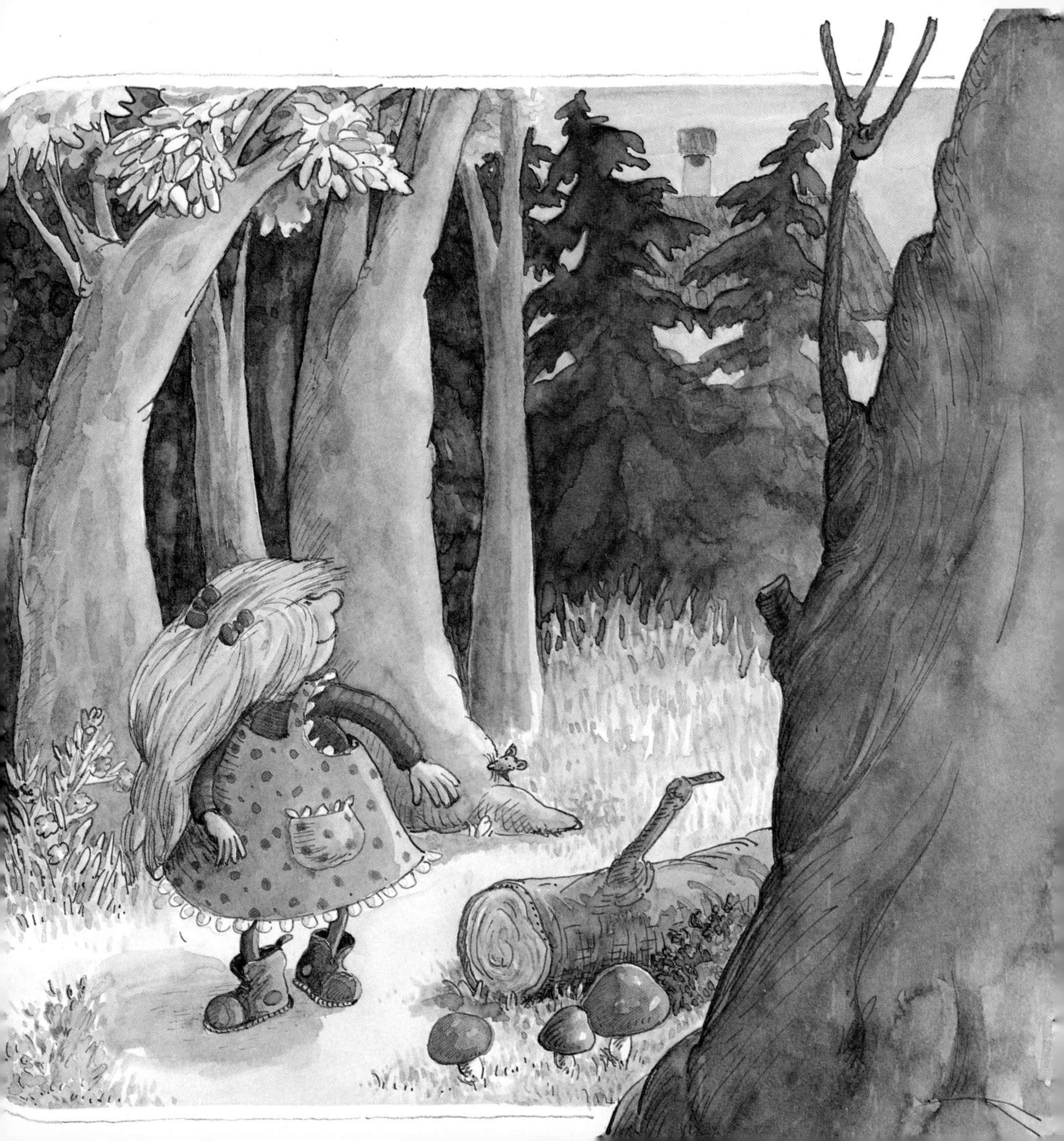

"Hello?" she shouted. "May I come in?"

Nobody answered, so she walked right in. Inside, everything was spotless and tidy. Goldilocks saw a table that seemed to be set for a meal. It had three chairs around it and three bowls on it. She went to the first chair, but it was much too hard. Then she tried the second chair, which had a big, fluffy cushion on its seat. But it was much too soft. Finally she climbed up on the third chair. It was just right.

"Mmm, this soup looks yummy," she said, licking her lips. "If I have just a drop, I don't think anyone will mind."

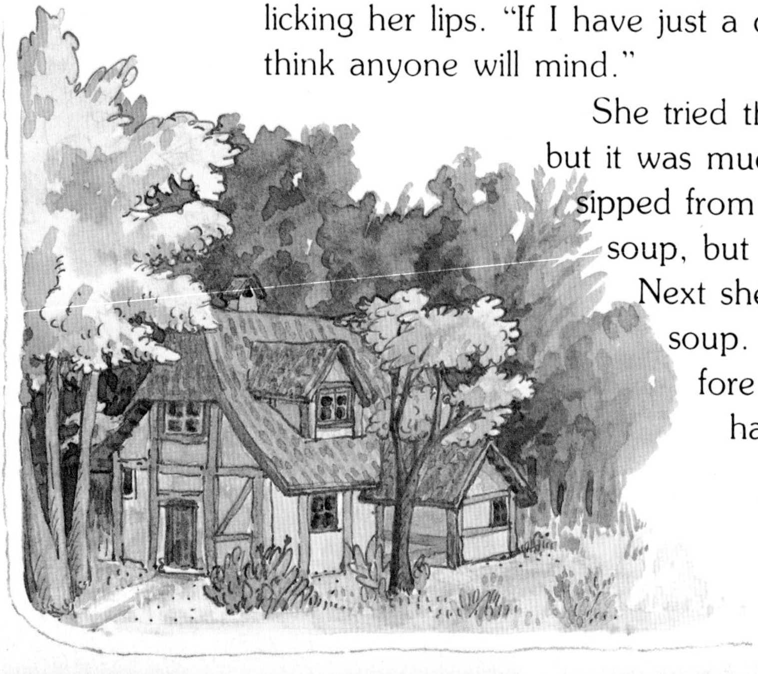

She tried the first bowl of soup, but it was much too hot. Then she sipped from the second bowl of soup, but it was much too cold. Next she tried the third bowl of soup. It was just right. Before she knew it, Goldilocks had gobbled it all up.

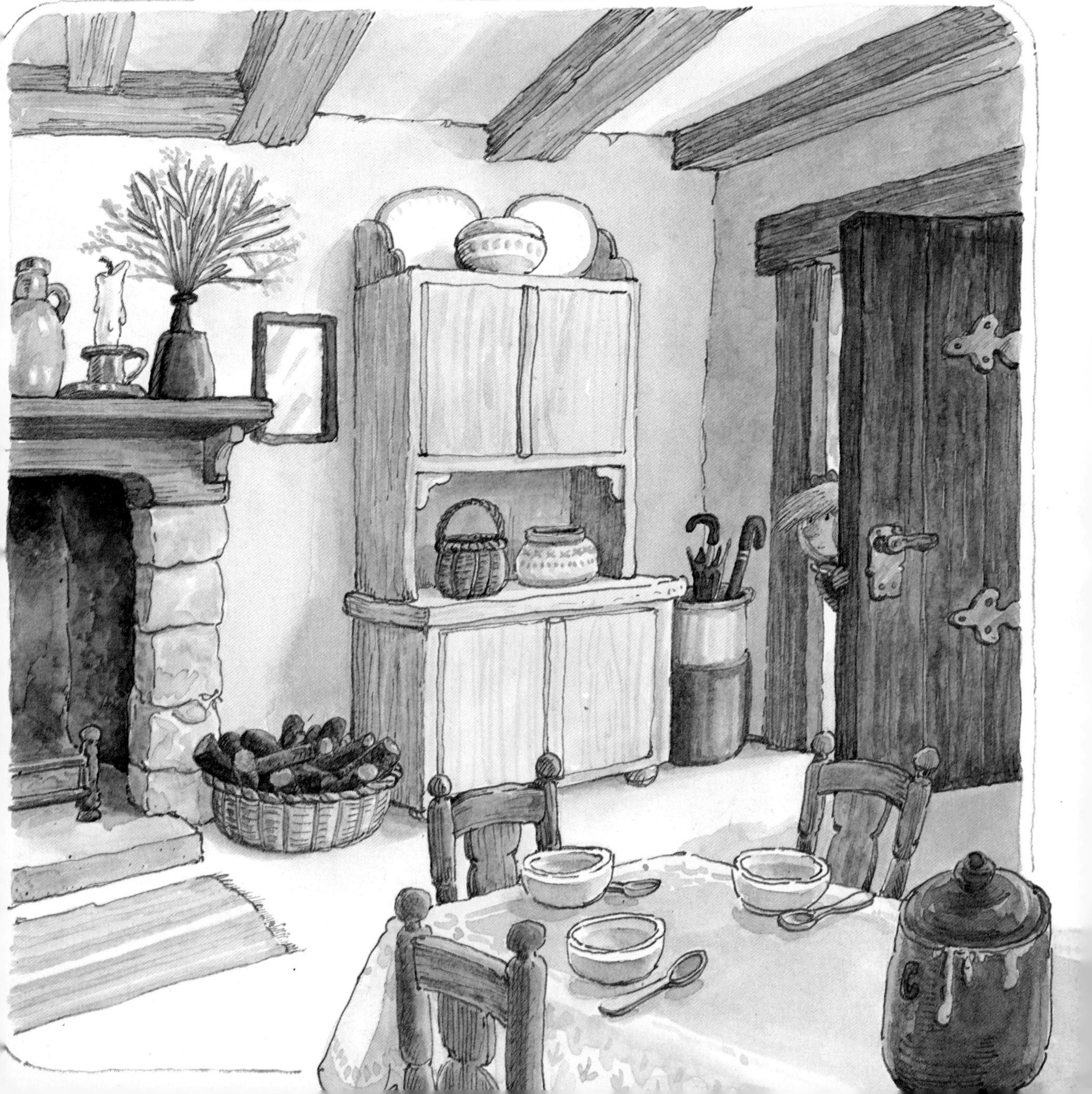

"Oh, I feel so sleepy," said Goldilocks when she had finished the soup. She felt her eyes closing, as she usually took a nap in the afternoon.

So Goldilocks found her way to the bedroom, where she saw three beds. First she tried the largest bed, but it was much too hard. Then she tried the middle bed, but it was much too soft. At last she tried the little bed. It was just right. She crawled under the covers and fell right to sleep.

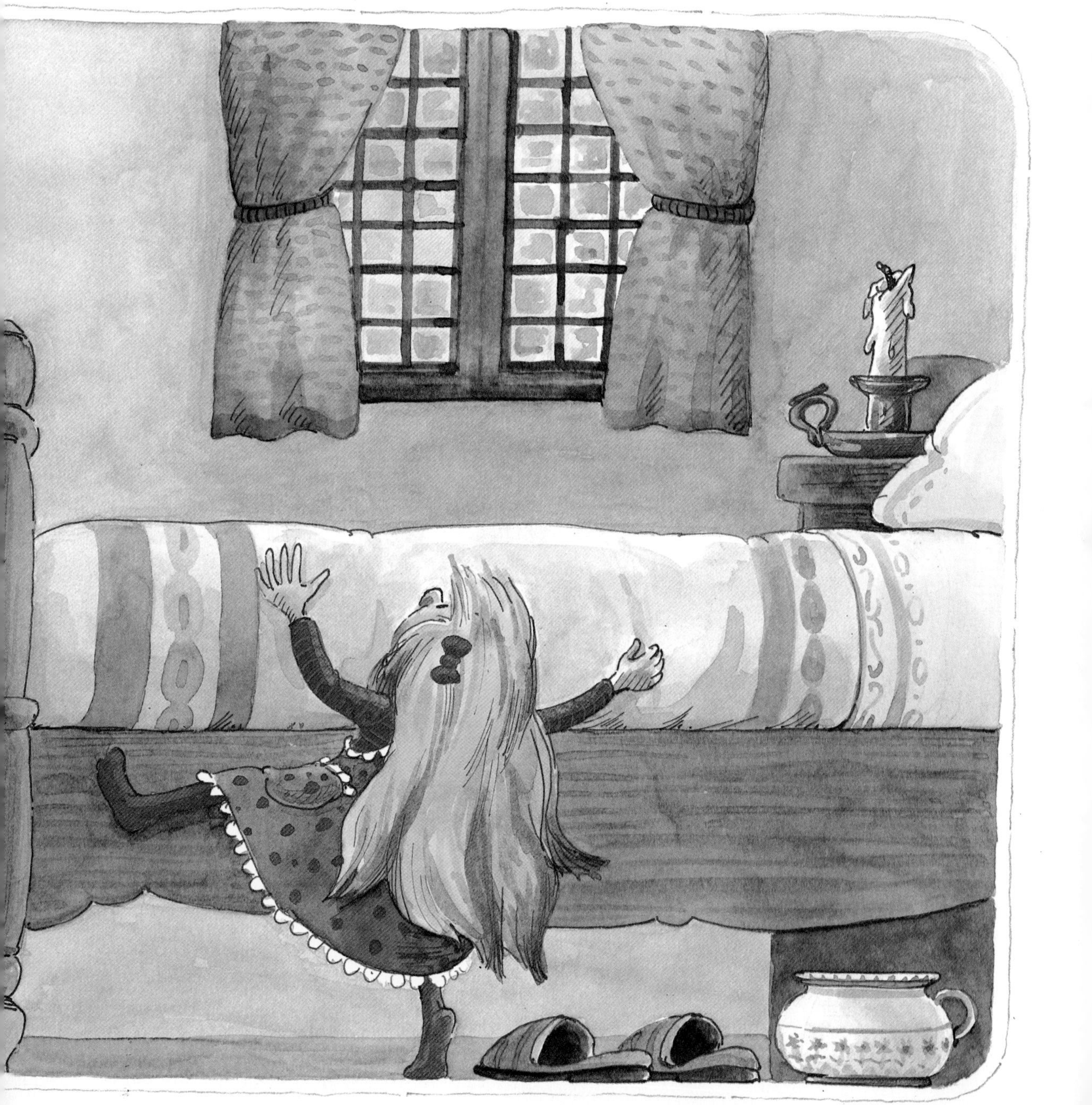

Just then, who do you suppose came home? It was the Bear family! Father Bear, Mother Bear, and Baby Bear. Father Bear knew right away that something was wrong.

"Someone's been sitting in my chair!" he said.

"And someone's been sitting in my chair!" said Mother Bear.

"Someone's been sitting in my chair and that someone has eaten all my soup!" cried Baby Bear in surprise.

Suddenly, the three Bears heard a soft, snoring sound. They followed the sound into the bedroom.

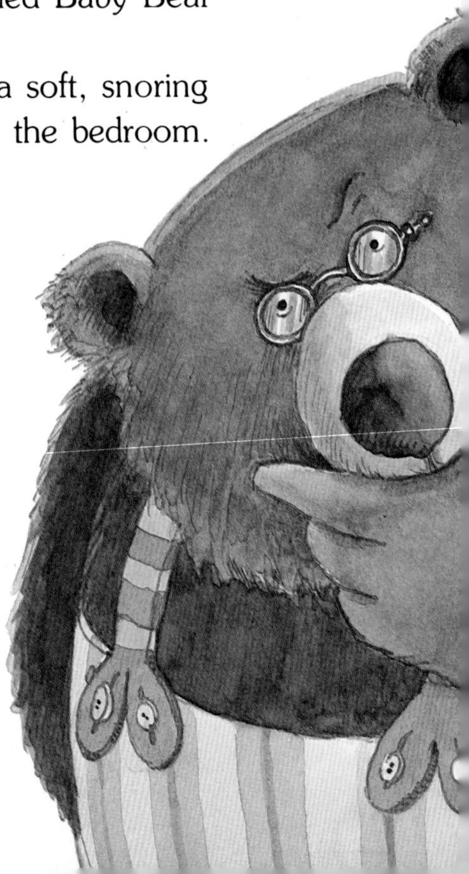

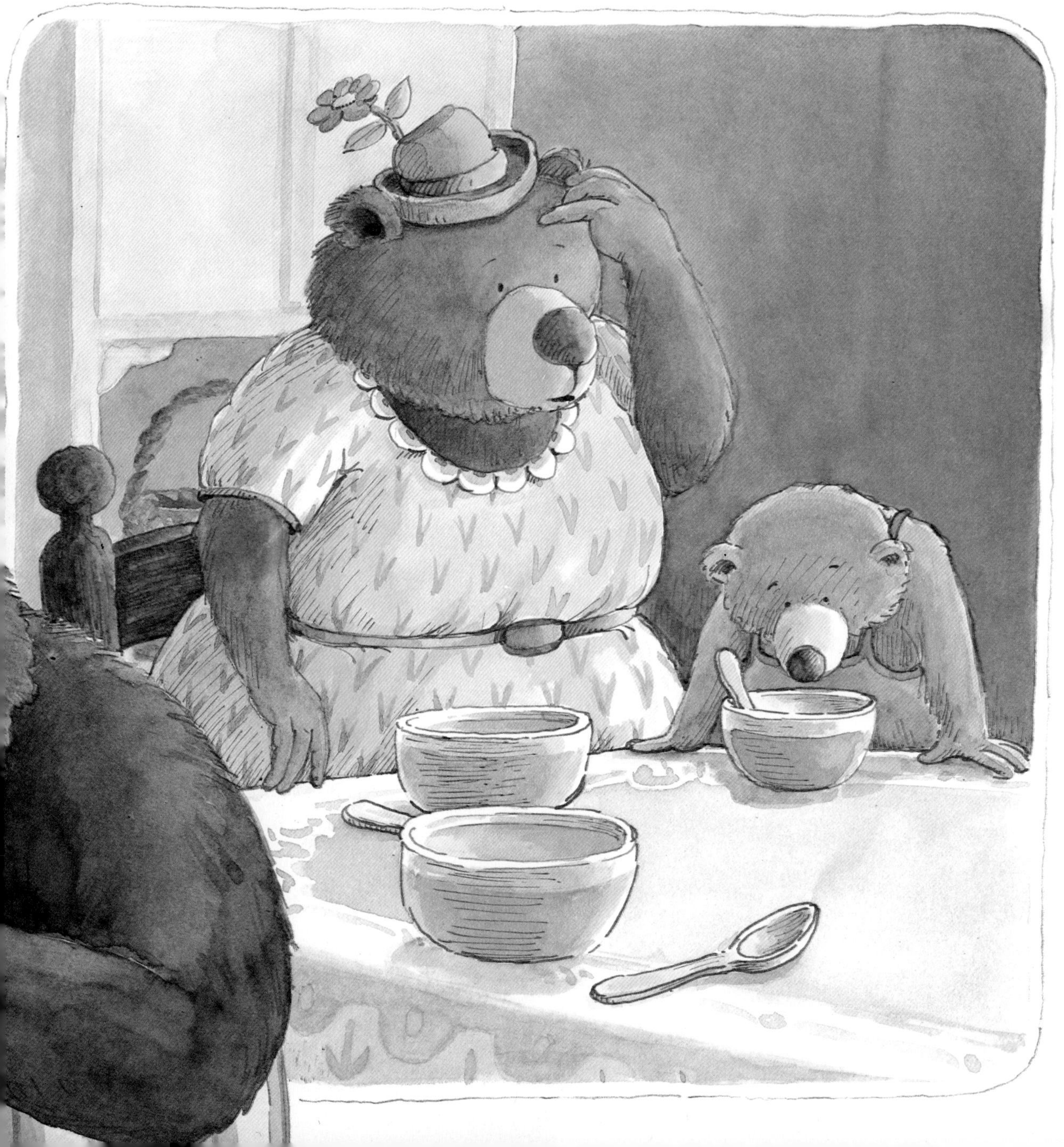

Father Bear took one look at his bed and saw right away that the blankets were in a mess.

"Someone's been sleeping in my bed!" he said.

"And someone's been sleeping in my bed!" said Mother Bear.

"Someone's been sleeping in my bed, and that someone is still there!" cried Baby Bear, pointing to Goldilocks.

"It's a little girl!" said Mother Bear.

"And a very naughty little girl," said Father Bear.

Just then, Goldilocks opened her eyes. You can imagine how scared she was! She saw three hairy faces looking down at her, and she screamed in fright.

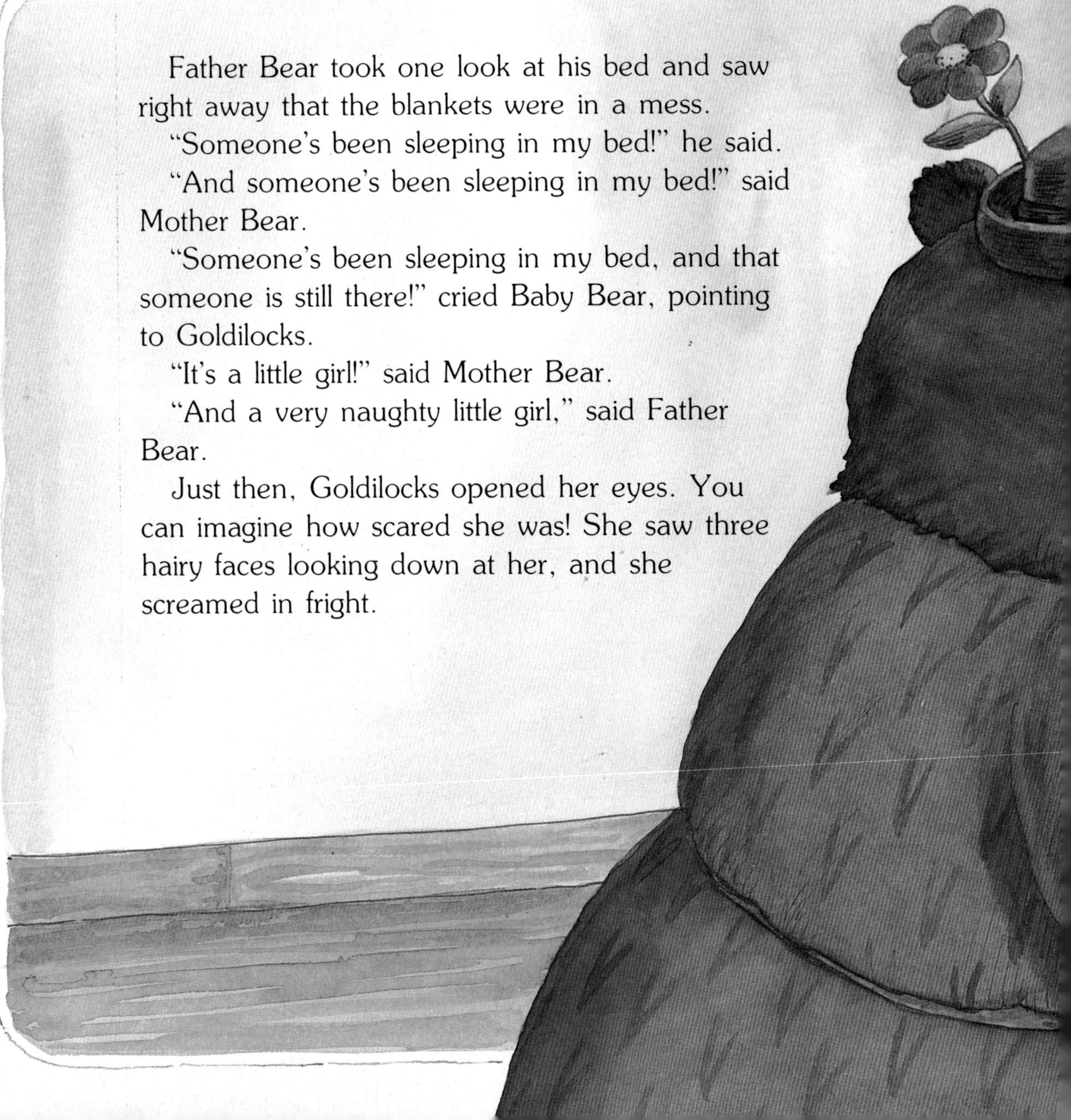

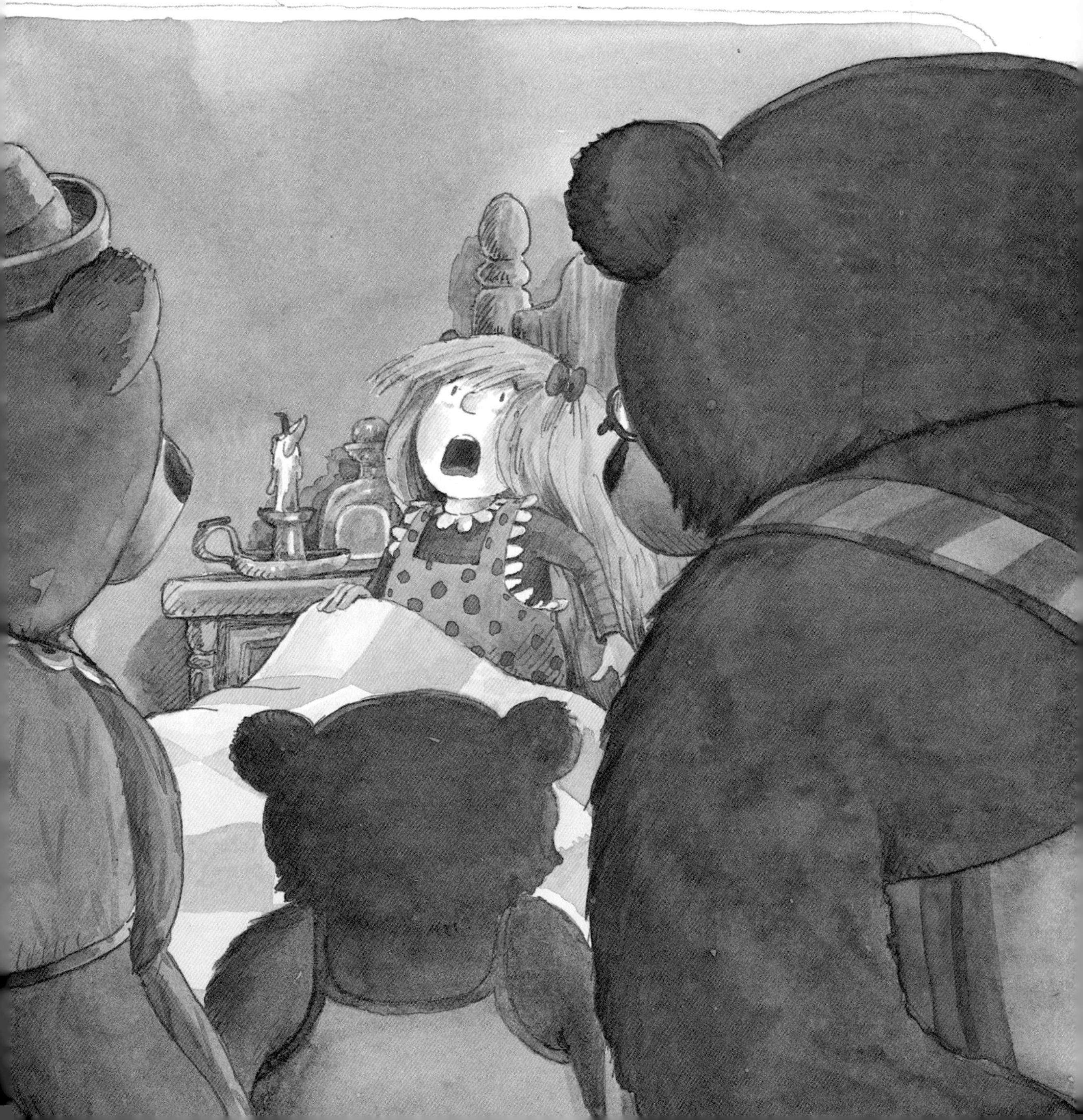

Father Bear was very angry. "Who are you and what are you doing here?" he asked.

"Oh!" cried Goldilocks. "These are the dangers that Mother warned me about!"

"What dangers? Who is a danger?" asked Mother Bear.

But Goldilocks was crying so hard that she could not answer.

Baby Bear was happy to see this stranger, for he did not have many friends in the woods to play with. "Oh Mother, Father, please let her stay!" he said.

"What do you mean, let her stay?" said Father Bear angrily. "People have to be with people and bears with bears."

"Oh p-p-please," cried Goldilocks, "I want to go home! My mother will be so worried!"

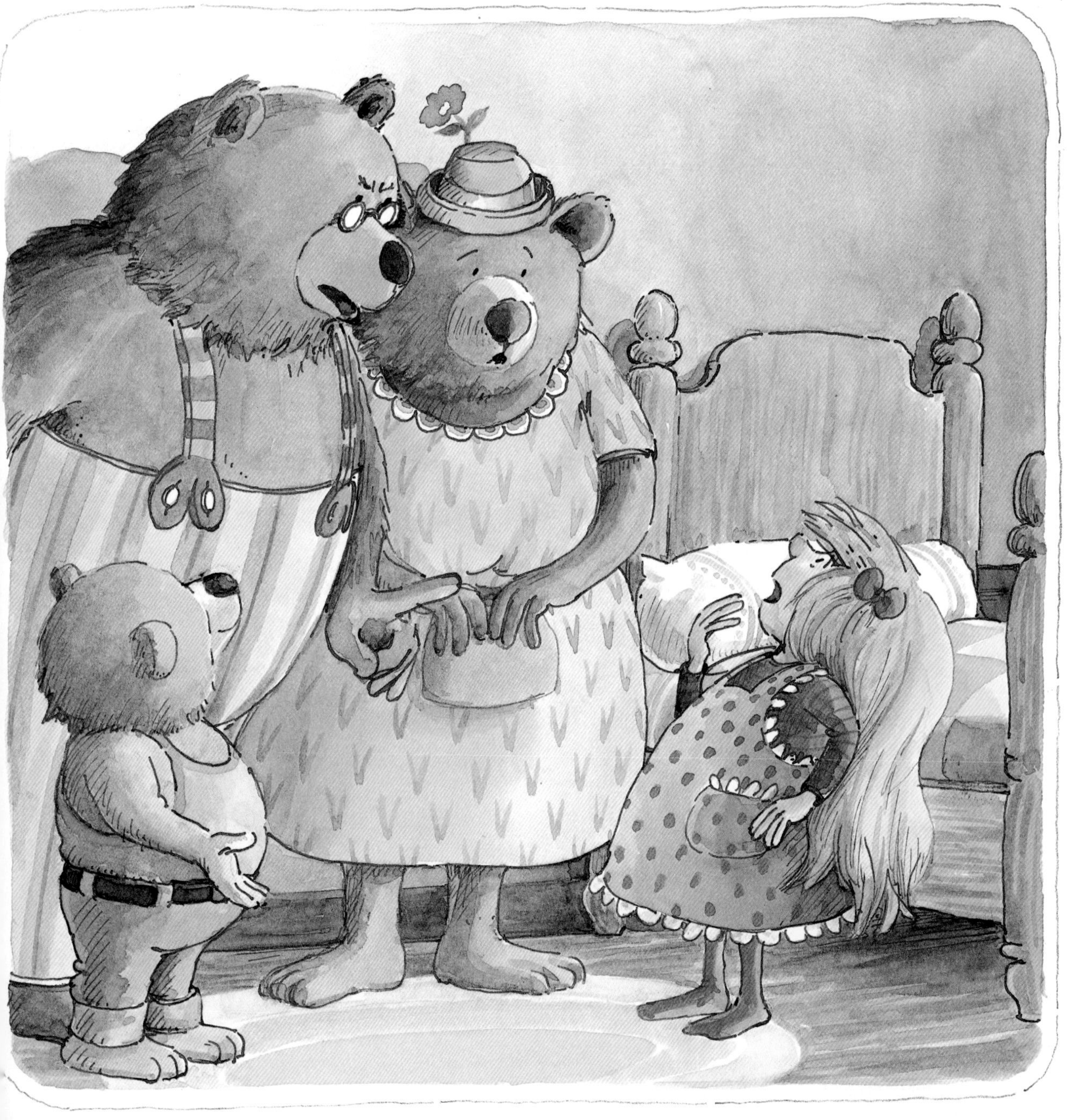

Mother Bear felt sorry for the pretty little girl. She stroked her golden hair and said, "There, there. Don't cry. Our son will take you home by a shortcut, and you will be there in no time."

"And from now on, don't go sneaking around in strangers' homes, eating their soup!" scolded Father Bear.

"I promise I won't," said Goldilocks. "Please forgive me, Mr. and Mrs. Bear."

Then she took Baby Bear's paw, and the two of them went out into the woods. The shortcut was very quick, and Goldilocks was home in a moment.

Baby Bear looked at her sadly and said, "You'll come back, won't you? We could play . . ."

"I don't know if my mother will let me," said Goldilocks. "But I'll try."

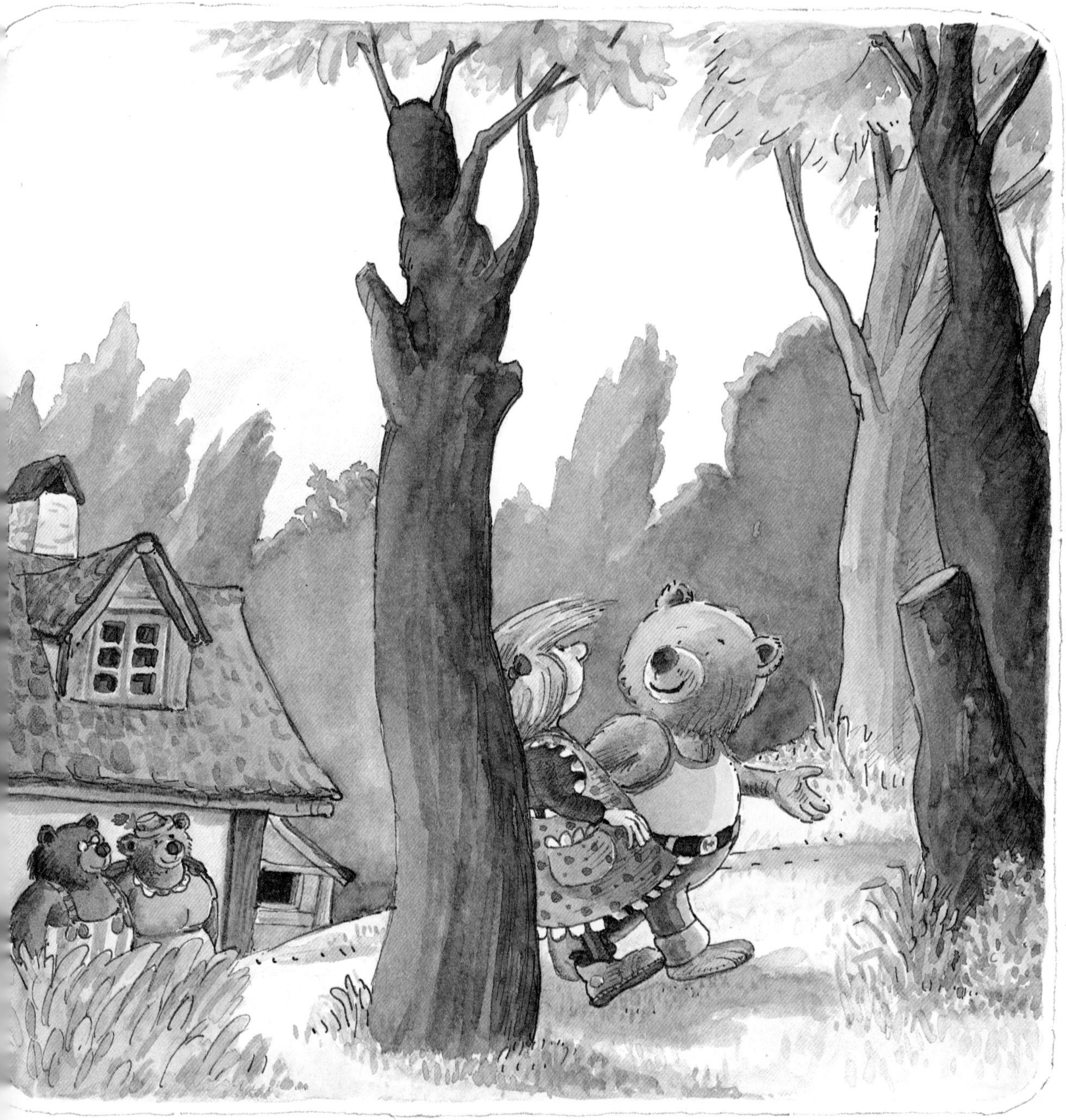

Goldilocks' mother was so happy to see her, she gave her a great big hug. But after the hug, she scolded her. "Where have you been all this time? I've searched the whole village for you."

Goldilocks had sworn never to lie to her mother again, so she told her about her adventure in the woods and her meeting with the three bears.

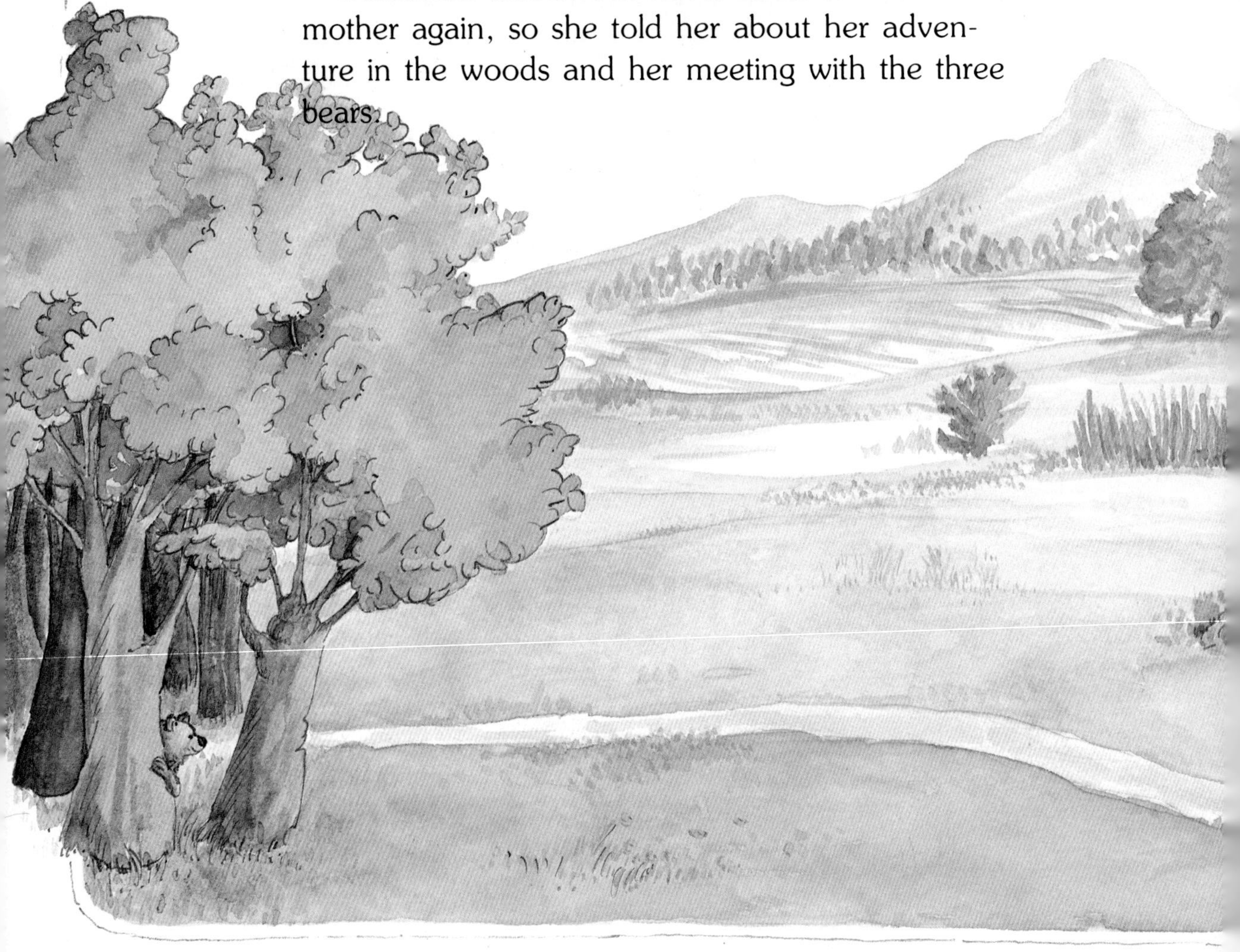

She added that the bears were not at all dangerous and that she would like to go back from time to time to play with Baby Bear.

"Well, that sounds like a tall story you've made up!" said her mother. She didn't quite believe her daughter's strange tale.

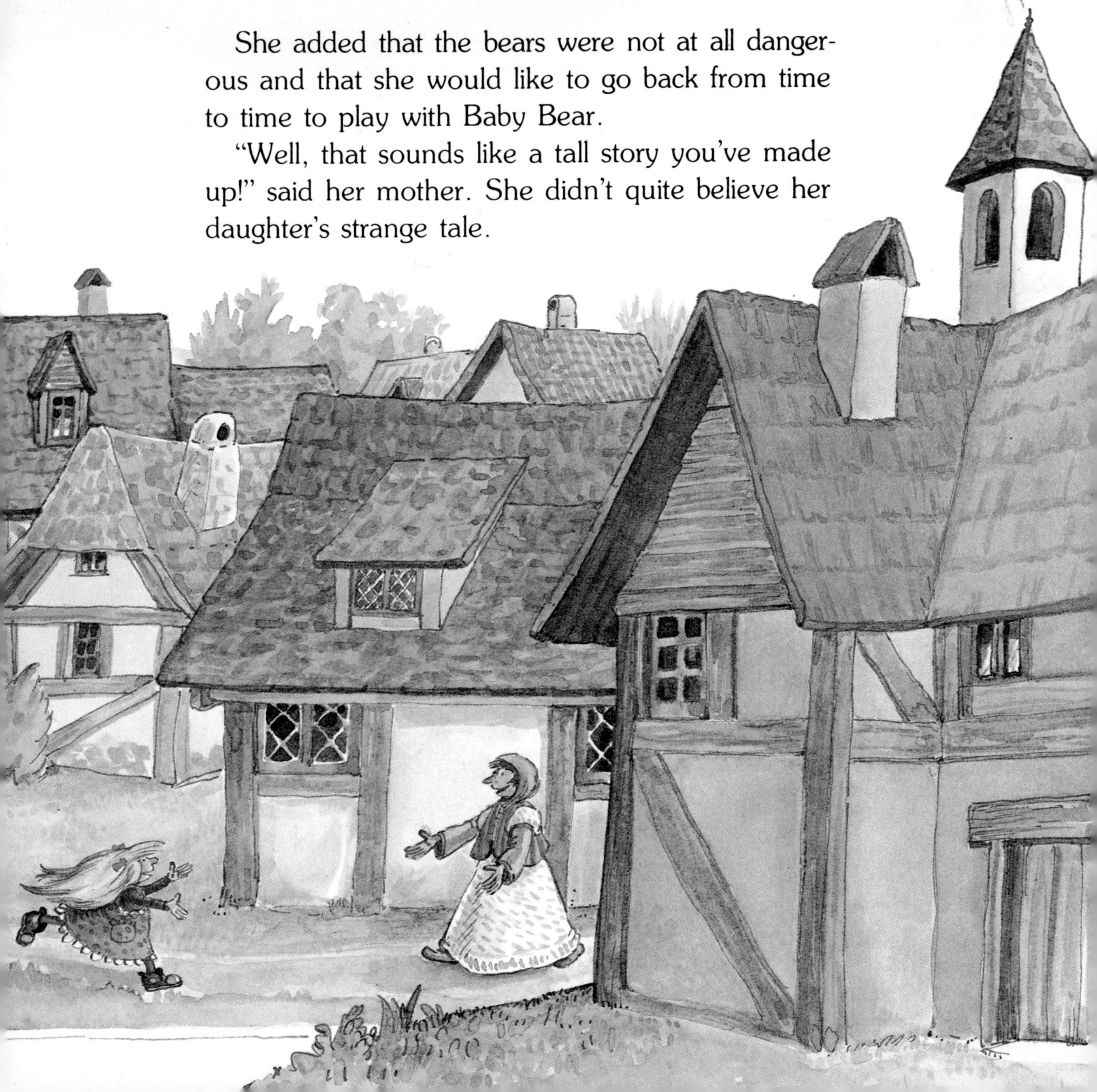

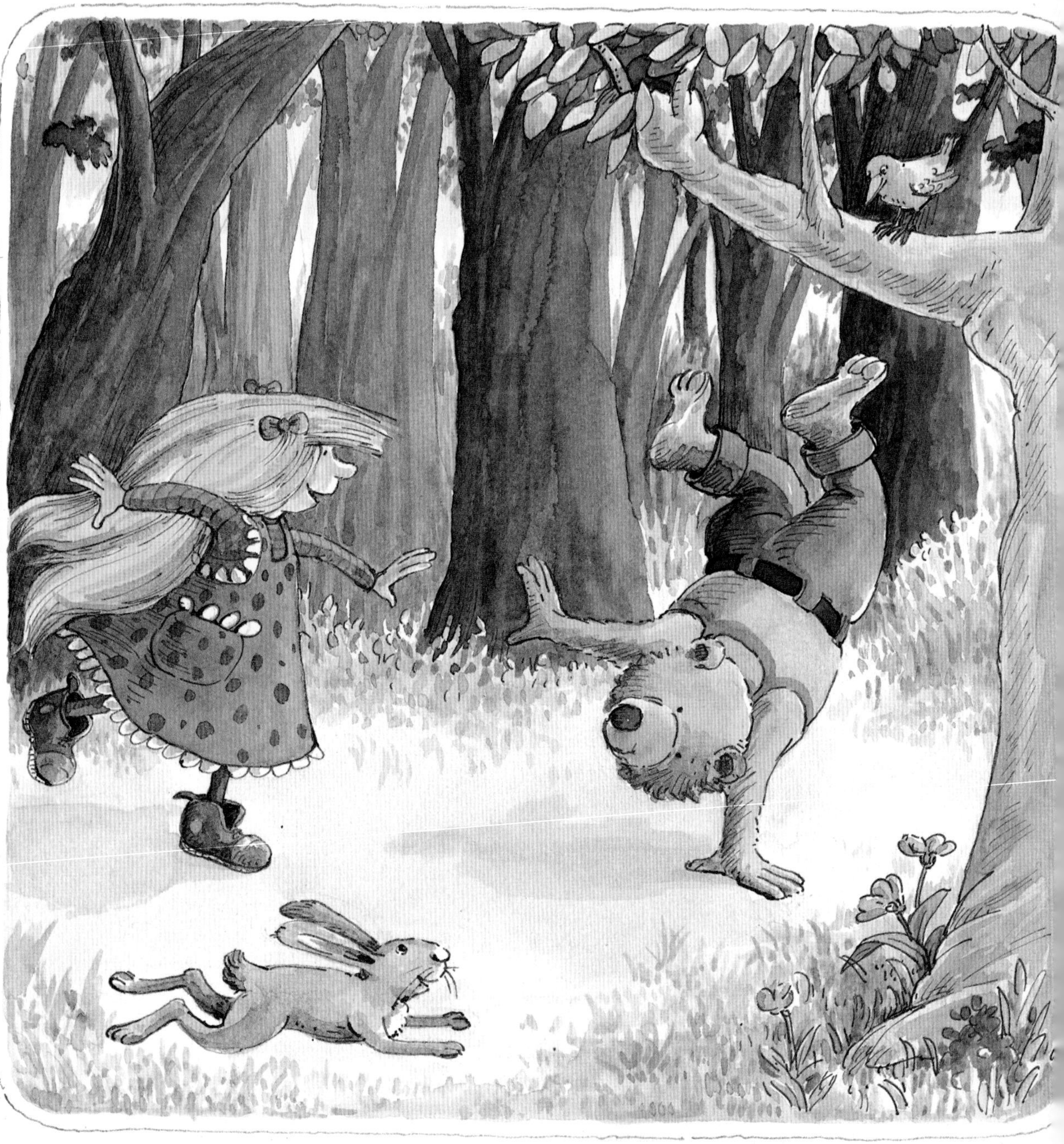

"It's true!" said Goldilocks. "Come with me to the woods and you will see for yourself." And that is just what Goldilocks' mother did.

So it was from that day on that Goldilocks visited the woods quite often. As time went by, Goldilocks became such good friends with Baby Bear that when they grew up, they had houses built next to each other.